The Gingerbread Man

A Favorite Story in Rhythm and Rhyme

Retold by SUSAN SANDVIG WALKER

Illustrated by VILLIE KARABATZIA

Music Arranged and Produced by MUSICAL YOUTH PRODUCTIONS

CANTATA LEARNING

WWW.CANTATALEARNING.COM

CANTATA
LEARNING

Published by Cantata Learning
1710 Roe Crest Drive
North Mankato, MN 56003
www.cantatalearning.com

A note to educators and librarians from the publisher: Cantata Learning has provided the following data to assist in book processing and suggested use of Cantata Learning product.

Publisher's Cataloging-in-Publication Data
Prepared by Librarian Consultant: Ann-Marie Begnaud
Library of Congress Control Number: 2015958220
    The Gingerbread Man: A Favorite Story in Rhythm and Rhyme
    Series: Fairy Tale Tunes
    Retold by Susan Sandvig Walker
    Illustrated by Villie Karabatzia
    Summary: The classic fairy tale of the Gingerbread Man comes to life with music and full-color illustrations.
    ISBN: 978-1-63290-555-0 (library binding/CD)
    ISBN: 978-1-63290-574-1 (paperback/CD)
Suggested Dewey and Subject Headings:
    Dewey: E 398.2
    LCSH Subject Headings: Fables – Juvenile literature. | Fables – Songs and music – Texts. | Fables – Juvenile sound recordings.
    Sears Subject Headings: Fables. | School songbooks. | Children's songs. | Jazz music.
    BISAC Subject Headings: JUVENILE FICTION / Fairy Tales & Folklore / Adaptations. | JUVENILE FICTION / Stories in Verse. | JUVENILE FICTION / Cooking & Food.

Book design and art direction, Tim Palin Creative
Editorial direction, Flat Sole Studio
Music direction, Elizabeth Draper
Music arranged and produced by Musical Youth Productions

Printed in the United States of America in North Mankato, Minnesota.
102016   0348CGF16R

All around the world, people have told tales about runaway food. The types of food change from place to place. In Europe, there are tales of runaway pancakes. In the United States, the stories are about a cookie shaped like a man.

To find out what happens
when this cookie makes
a run for it, turn the page
and sing along!

A little old woman
and a little old man
baked a sweet little gingery
gingerbread man.

When the oven popped open,
much to their surprise,
he jumped up and ran
right before their eyes.

Run, run, run as fast as you can.

You can't catch me.

I'm the Gingerbread Man!

I ran from your oven
and your little house, too.
I'll outrun every one of you!

He ran and ran
through a field of hay,
where a cow mooed,
"Cookieman, come my way."

Some piggies trotted
toward the Gingerbread Man, too.
But he was much too fast
for that four-legged **crew**.

Run, run, run as fast as you can.

You can't catch me.

I'm the Gingerbread Man!

I ran from a cow
and some piggies, too.
I'll outrun every one of you!

He ran to a school,
where the kids all play,
and the boys and the girls
all **skipped** his way.

They tried to get a bite
of that tasty cookie man.
But he skipped, and he hopped,
and away he ran.

Run, run, run as fast as you can.

You can't catch me.

I'm the Gingerbread Man!

I ran from some boys
and from some girls, too
I'll outrun every one of you!

He ran to a river,
so fast and wide,
where a **sly** little fox
offered him a ride.

18

The fox swam across,
the cookie on his back,
and then **gobbled** him up
for a gingerbread snack.

Run, run, run as fast as you can.

A fox is smarter
than the Gingerbread Man,
who ran from the oven,
and he wouldn't stop.

But he couldn't outrun that tricky fox!

SONG LYRICS
The Gingerbread Man

A little old woman
and a little old man
baked a sweet little gingery
gingerbread man.

When the oven popped open,
much to their surprise,
he jumped up and ran
right before their eyes.

Run, run, run as fast as you can.
You can't catch me.
I'm the Gingerbread Man!

I ran from your oven
and your little house, too.
I'll outrun every one of you!

He ran and ran
through a field of hay,
where a cow mooed,
"Cookieman, come my way."

Some piggies trotted
toward the Gingerbread Man, too.
But he was much too fast
for that four-legged crew.

Run, run, run as fast as you can.
You can't catch me.
I'm the Gingerbread Man!

I ran from a cow
and some piggies, too.
I'll outrun every one of you!

He ran to a school,
where the kids all play,
and the boys and the girls
all skipped his way.

They tried to get a bite
of that tasty cookie man.
But he skipped, and he hopped,
and away he ran.

Run, run, run as fast as you can.
You can't catch me.
I'm the Gingerbread Man!

I ran from some boys
and from some girls, too.
I'll outrun every one of you!

He ran to a river,
so fast and wide,
where a sly little fox
offered him a ride.

The fox swam across,
the cookie on his back,
and then gobbled him up
for a gingerbread snack.

Run, run, run as fast as you can.
A fox is smarter
than the Gingerbread Man,
who ran from the oven,
and he wouldn't stop.
But he couldn't outrun that
tricky fox.

The Gingerbread Man

Jazz
Musical Youth Productions

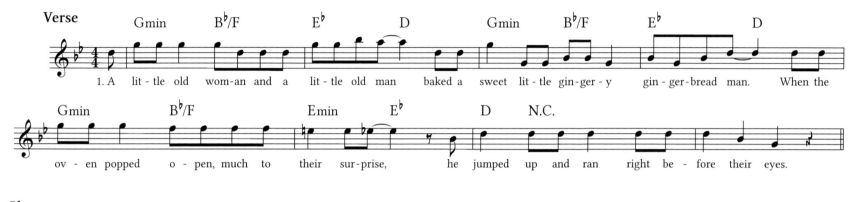

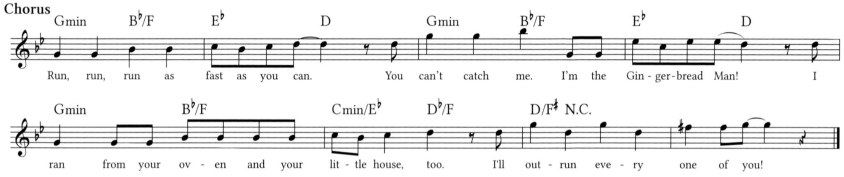

Verse 2
He ran and ran through a field of hay,
where a cow mooed, "Cookieman, come my way."
Some piggies trotted toward the Gingerbread Man, too.
But he was much too fast for that four-legged crew.

Chorus
Run, run, run as fast as you can.
You can't catch me. I'm the Gingerbread Man!
I ran from a cow and some piggies, too.
I'll outrun every one of you!

Verse 3
He ran to a school, where the kids all play,
and the boys and the girls all skipped his way.
They tried to get a bite of that tasty cookie man.
But he skipped, and he hopped, and away he ran.

Chorus
Run, run, run as fast as you can.
You can't catch me. I'm the Gingerbread Man!
I ran from some boys and from some girls, too.
I'll outrun every one of you!

Verse 4
He ran to a river, so fast and wide,
where a sly little fox offered him a ride.
The fox swam across, the cookie on his back,
and then gobbled him up for a gingerbread snack.

Chorus
Run, run, run as fast as you can.
A fox is smarter than the Gingerbread Man,
who ran from the oven, and he wouldn't stop.
But he couldn't outrun that tricky fox.

GLOSSARY

crew—a team of people who work on something together

gingerbread—a cake or cookie flavored with ginger and other spices

gobbled—ate something quickly and greedily

skipped—moved along in a bouncy way, hopping on each foot in turn

sly—sneaky and clever

GUIDED READING ACTIVITIES

1. Have you ever eaten gingerbread? If so, did you like how it tasted?

2. The gingerbread man runs from everyone except the fox. Was that a good idea? Why or why not?

3. With a brown crayon or marker, draw the shape of a gingerbread man or woman on a piece of paper. Use crayons or markers and your imagination to decorate your gingerbread person.

TO LEARN MORE

Braun, Eric, Nancy Loewen, and Trisha Speed Shaskan. *The Other Side of the Story: Fairy Tales from a Different Perspective.* North Mankato, MN: Picture Window Books, a Capstone imprint, 2014.

Kimmel, Erik. The *Runaway Tortilla.* Portland, OR: WestWinds Press, 2015.

Murray, Laura. *The Gingerbread Man Loose at the Zoo.* New York: G. P. Putnam's Sons.

Robinson, Hillary. *Three Pigs and a Gingerbread Man.* New York: Crabtree, 2013.